My Stepfather Shrank!

Also by Barbara Dillon
Mrs. Tooey and the Terrible Toxic Tar
A Mom by Magic

My Stepfather Shrank!

by Barbara Dillon

illustrated by Paul Casale

HarperCollins*Publishers*

My Stepfather Shrank!

Typography by Joyce Hopkins
1 2 3 4 5 6 7 8 9 10
First Edition

Library of Congress Cataloging-in-Publication Data
Dillon, Barbara.
My stepfather shrank! / by Barbara Dillon ; illustrated by Paul Casale.
    p.   cm.
    Summary: Nine-year-old Mallory discovers that her new stepfather has been accidentally shrunk and tries to return him to normal size before her mother gets home.
    ISBN 0-06-021574-7. — ISBN 0-06-021581-X (lib. bdg.)
    [1. Size—Fiction.   2. Stepfathers—Fiction.   3. Science fiction.]   I. Casale, Paul, ill.   II. Title.
PZ7.D57916My   1992   91-23901
[Fic]—dc20   CIP
                                                                        AC

For Emily

Contents

My Stepfather Shrank!

1

The Shrinking

MALLORY WATSON STOOD gloomily in the hallway listening to her mother, who was giving last-minute instructions to her stepfather.

"I hate leaving you two," she was saying, her eyes straying to Mallory, "and I wouldn't do it if Aunt Karen didn't need me to help with the new baby."

She paused, waiting for either Mallory or

Woody to say that it was okay, they'd manage just fine. As far as Mallory was concerned, nothing about staying alone for the weekend with her new stepfather was fine. He had a nerdy nickname, Woody, and an even nerdier full name, Elwood Sherman, and that was only the beginning of his nerdiness. She gave her mother a stony stare and silently scratched a mosquito bite, the first of the season, on her elbow. But Woody finally relented and with a brave smile said, "We'll manage, Gretchen. Just go and have a good time."

"And you'll be okay without your car?" her mother asked uncertainly.

"Nelson's garage said they'd have it ready for me by tomorrow afternoon," Woody told her. "Then I thought Mal and I could go marketing for a little steak to cook out on the grill." He glanced at Mallory with the slightly baffled look he always gave her, as though a nine-year-old belonged to an entirely different species.

"Oh, how nice," Mrs. Sherman said, sounding pleased.

He'll never be able to get the fire going without Mom's help, Mallory thought with glum satisfaction. Then I'll have to go to bed hungry and it'll serve Mom right.

"And there I'll be down in New Jersey warming bottles and changing diapers," her mother said with a rueful smile. But Mallory knew she was really excited about seeing Aunt Karen's baby.

With a martyred sigh Mallory raised her face for a farewell kiss. She stood at the front door scratching her mosquito bite and frowning through the screen as Woody carried her mother's bag out to the driveway. She watched the two of them talking earnestly; from the way they glanced back at the house, Mallory felt sure she was being discussed. Her mother was so anxious for her and Woody to get to know each other better. Her mother and Woody had been married for almost six months now—five months and twenty-one days. Mallory was keeping careful track. Mallory felt she knew Woody well enough to be sure that absolutely nothing could ever make her glad of his presence. She and her mother had been doing just fine on their own. She watched Woody put her mother's suitcase in the back of the car and kiss her good-bye; not just a peck but a real kiss, as if she were going off for two months rather than two days. For Pete's sake! thought Mallory. Woody stood at the top of the driveway, following the blue station wagon with his eyes all the way down Pilgrim Road. So did Mallory. When it was out of sight, he turned resolutely toward the house. As he opened the screen door, Mallory announced in a firm voice, "I think I'll ride my bike into town."

This was something she didn't even bother to ask her mother for permission to do. She knew that Mrs. Sherman thought that the traffic on the Post Road was too heavy for a nine-year-old to handle. Mallory could ride down to the newsstand at the corner, but the center of town was definitely off limits.

Woody looked at her dubiously. "Do you think it would be all right with your mom?" he asked.

"Oh yes," Mallory assured him. "She wouldn't mind. I'm going upstairs to get my money."

Her plan was to ride to Becker's Pharmacy. After twenty-five years the store was going out of business and there were to be "drastic reductions on all merchandise."

In her bedroom Mallory removed the rubber plug from the bottom of her Mickey Mouse bank and counted out six dollars in bills. She folded them into a tight square to fit into the little tooled leather purse that she slung around her neck. The remaining money, all in quarters, she placed in the back pocket of her jeans.

When she emerged from the house, Woody was trying unsuccessfully to get the lawn mower started. Even her father, who had traveled so much on business that he was scarcely ever at home to do yardwork, hadn't had the trouble Woody did.

"Woody was a city boy, don't forget," Mallory's mother had reminded her more than once. Well, that wasn't a good enough excuse for being a klutz, Mallory thought sternly, wheeling her bike from the garage. Nor was it an excuse for the way Woody dressed. Before he had moved in with them, he'd bought all these special outfits for "the country," as he had referred to Jefferson Village. Slacks were perfectly coordinated with shirts and sweaters. His jeans were spotless; his sneakers gleamed. He looked so perfect he reminded Mallory of a department-store dummy.

He paused now in his labors to wave to her as she pedaled down the driveway. She gave him an indifferent wave back.

Out on the Post Road Mallory thought how silly it was of her mother not to permit her to ride into town. If she could see how skillfully her daughter handled a bike, she'd grant permission at once. Mallory was just sorry her best friend, Alison Beatty, wasn't with her. Because of the teachers' meeting today, school had closed at noon, so Alison had taken off with her parents for a visit with her grandparents. Alison's trip this weekend was bad timing. If her friend had been at home, Mallory would have spent every minute at her house, even sleeping over, so as to completely avoid being with Woody. As it was, she was stuck with him. He'd taken today off from work so her mother could get started for Aunt Karen's before rush hour on the highways.

In town, Mallory braked her bike in front of Becker's Pharmacy, the purse swinging around her neck as she dismounted. She glanced eagerly at the big banner in the window that said: "Going Out of Business. All Merchandise 30% to 50% Off."

As she entered the store, she was surprised to see a beautiful marmalade-colored kitten curled up on a pile of newspapers.

"You look like Mrs. Peebles' Alice," she told the cat, pausing to stroke it behind the ears, "only much tinier."

Mrs. Peebles herself was on duty at the cash register. Mr. Becker was talking on the telephone in back of the prescription counter.

"Did Alice have kittens, Mrs. Peebles?" Mallory asked, stepping aside to let two women customers by.

"Oh, hello there. No, that is Alice herself, Mallory," Mrs. Peebles called cheerily. Mrs. Peebles knew almost all of Mr. Becker's regular customers by name, just as they knew her first name was Loretta and that she had a sister who was in a soap opera on television. They also knew about her husband, Rudy, who was an inventor. One of his inventions had been a laundry soap guaranteed, he said, to remove the most stubborn stains. It also ate paint off windowsills. Mallory's mother had been given one of the trial bars that Mrs. Peebles had brought into the pharmacy, and there was still a damaged spot on the kitchen sill to prove it. Another Peebles invention had been a tartar-control toothpaste that had turned Mrs. Peebles' teeth green, though not permanently.

"But on damp days I think they still color up a bit," she would tell customers. "See, it was these wackadoo inventions that finally got to me. That's why I asked for the trial separation. Rudy and I are still good friends and I do miss him, but with that man the only thing you can expect is the unexpected. He keeps a person off balance, you know what I'm saying?"

"But, Mrs. Peebles, I saw Alice just last week and she was her normal size," Mallory persisted as she walked to the counter. "How could she have gotten so tiny in just seven days?"

"Well, cats do that sometimes," Mrs. Peebles replied vaguely. "Could I interest you in some nice cologne?" She reached around to a shelf behind her. "This Moroccan Nights is a real steal," she told Mallory. "A nine ninety-five value for only three eighty-nine. Put out your hand, honey." Mrs. Peebles leaned across the counter and sprayed the inside of Mallory's wrist with scent.

"Nice," Mallory said, taking a thoughtful sniff. Actually Moroccan Nights struck her as a bit strong, but the bottle was very pretty and would make a nice Christmas gift for her grandmother. Of course, December was seven months away. Still, when you came upon a good bargain like this, it was smart to grab it up, she thought, unsnapping her purse.

A customer approached the counter carrying a bottle of hair tonic, three boxes of tissues, and a packet of antacid tablets. Mrs. Peebles rang up his purchases on the cash register and put them in a plastic bag. "Have a nice one," she told him, and turned back to Mallory. "How about some Peebles Confections?" she asked. She reached past the perfume display to a wicker basket filled with plastic bags of candy.

Mallory was delighted to see them. Mrs. Peebles' homemade candy was delicious. In fact, Mallory had been hoping that today there would be a few sample pieces laid out, as there sometimes were, in a glass dish on the counter.

"I've scrambled up a couple of batches," Mrs. Peebles said. "You get a few pieces of chocolate fudge, some penuche, and a chocolate cream. At two fifty a bag, how can you go wrong?"

"Sure, I'll take one," Mallory said eagerly. As she reached into her purse again, her eye was caught by a display of hair bands, on sale like everything else. There was a particularly pretty one, black with gold braid on it. A perfect Christmas present for her friend Alison. Of course she didn't have too much money left after the purchase of the perfume, the candy, and now the hair band, but she was satisfied with what she'd bought.

While Mallory was counting out her change, Mr. Becker put down the telephone and waved.

"I'm glad you managed to get in today," he called to her. "It's our last full day of business. Can you imagine? After twenty-five years of standing behind this counter. Isn't that something?"

"I'll miss you, Mr. Becker," Mallory said, and meant it. The only other pharmacy in town was part of a large chain. It had four or five checkout counters and nobody knew you there; also there was not the assortment of interesting little gadgety things that Mr. Becker stocked, nor was there homemade candy.

"I'll miss you and Alice too," Mallory said to

Mrs. Peebles as she gathered up her purchases.

"Well, it's customers like you and your mom who kept Ed Becker in business all these years," Mrs. Peebles said warmly. "You have a nice day now.

"How ya doing, Mrs. Kleinschmidt?" she called to a middle-aged woman coming through the door. "We got that cough syrup you asked about the other day."

With a final curious glance at Alice, Mallory left the store and climbed back on her bike. As she pedaled along the Post Road, she thought of how many good-byes there were in life. The biggest for her had been when her dad left home and moved into an apartment in New York. And then her best friend before Alison, Emily Lauton, had moved away.

"I don't like anything to change," she muttered, giving a left-turn hand signal before pulling onto Elm Street. "I like everything to stay just the way it is."

When she arrived home, Woody was in the kitchen, a dish towel tucked into his trousers like an apron, heating up the hamburger casserole Mallory's mother had left.

"Supper's going to be ready shortly," he said. "Maybe you can set the table for us."

That was another thing that bothered Mallory about Woody—his insistence that they eat in the dining room, sometimes even with candles on the table. Before he had moved in with them, Mallory and her mother had dined cozily in the den in front of the TV. Now they had nerdy dinners in the dining room, and besides all that, they had to wait till seven-fifteen every night to eat because Woody's train didn't get in till quarter of. The only reason dinner was early tonight was because he hadn't gone in to work.

As Mallory took the place mats and the silverware from the sideboard, she became aware of a burning smell coming from the kitchen; a moment later she heard the sizzle of a pan being put under the cold-water faucet in the sink.

"That's the end of the string beans," Woody reported ruefully. "The water boiled away. I hope the pan isn't ruined."

So dinner was her mother's casserole and a tomato-and-lettuce salad, also some pretty good rolls from the bakery. It was a wonder Woody hadn't burned those too when he'd warmed them in the oven. The conversation, such as it was, went in little fits and starts. Woody wondered if Mallory's mother had run into any traffic on the way to New Jersey. He hoped she hadn't. He also hoped the weather would be pleasant tomorrow. Mallory said she thought it would probably rain. Woody asked her where she had gone in town and she told him she had done some Christmas shopping at Becker's. He seemed amused by that. "Well, you'll beat the last-minute rush, that's for sure," he said.

"What's for dessert?" Mallory asked, hoping her mother had made a butterscotch pudding before she left.

Woody regarded her blankly. "I don't know," he said, "but I think there're some chocolate chip cookies in the bread box."

"Those tired old things," Mallory said crossly. And then she remembered her candy from Becker's. She went out to the hall, where she had left the package, returning a second later with the bag in her hand.

"Would you like a piece?" she asked Woody in the coldly distant voice she reserved for Jerry Doolittle, the dork who sat in back of her in math.

"Oh thanks, I can never resist butter creams, which is what that one looks like," Woody said, reaching through the mouth of the bag. "Unless," he hesitated, "you'd like it."

"No, it's okay," Mallory said, glad that he hadn't chosen the penuche, which was her favorite. She picked out one of those from the bag. With her free hand she carried her dinner plate with the knife and fork and milk glass balanced precariously on top into the kitchen. She set the plate in the sink and popped the penuche into her mouth, savoring the delightful brown-sugar taste. A moment or two later Woody came through the swinging kitchen door carrying his plate. She gave him an indifferent glance but then looked again. It was silly, but he looked shorter to her. How could that possibly be? He was a tall man, almost six feet, her mother said, and yet at that moment he certainly appeared shorter. In fact as he put his plate on the counter, she noticed that the sleeves of his pullover reached almost to his knuckles.

"I didn't realize this sweater had stretched so," he said, observing his arms in surprise. "Look at these sleeves." He pushed them back up his arms, and as he did so his gold wedding band slipped off his finger and rolled to the floor.

"Well, if that isn't the weirdest thing," he said, bending to retrieve it. "This ring's always been a little on the snug side." Looking puzzled, he went back to the dining room for the butter dish and the salt and pepper shakers. Mallory, deciding not to save the other piece of penuche for a pre-bedtime snack as she had originally planned, took a generous bite from it. Then she ate the remaining bit as she stood gazing out the kitchen window at the new spring grass, green as garden peas in the twilight. She glanced down at her watch. Almost time for *Love Triangle*, a show her mother never allowed her to watch, but Woody probably didn't know that. Now was a good opportunity to see it.

As she passed through the dining room on her way to the den, she was surprised to see Woody's clothes lying in a heap on the rug. Baffled, she stepped around them, wondering if he had gone upstairs. But if he had, why wouldn't he have taken the clothes with him? And why would he have undressed in the dining room?

Then she heard it: a tiny, tinny voice. "Mallory, help!" it called. It seemed to be coming from the pile of discarded clothes. She squatted down to examine them more closely.

One of Woody's shirt sleeves was twitching as though perhaps a mouse were buried beneath it. Mallory half expected to see a pair of little ears appear above the cuff. In fact that was what she did see, but not mouse ears—human ears—Woody's ears. Between them was his tiny agitated face. His blue eyes were mere pinpricks; his mouth, opened in surprise and horror, was about as big as the hole in a Cheerio. You had to squint to see that his brown hair even had curls in it, they were so small. Two teeny hands grasped the arm of the shirt, gathering it up around his naked shoulders.

"Mallory, I've shrunk!" Woody cried. "I was afraid you were going to step on me! I don't know how this has happened. It can't have happened. Tell me I'm just having a nightmare."

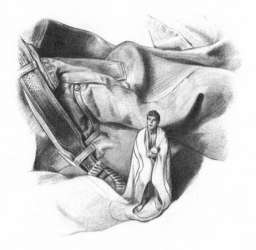

2

Shrunken

"OH WOODY!" Mallory could think of nothing else to say. Her first instinct was to pick him up, but he shied away from her outstretched hand, clutching the shirt sleeve around him.

"I have nothing on," he stammered. "I shrank right out of my clothes."

Mallory could not take her eyes off the terrified upturned face. And then a chill went through her as she thought of her mother. What would she say when she came home on Sunday and found her new husband no bigger than the father in Mallory's dollhouse family? Would she somehow blame Mallory for the disaster?

"Mr. Hemingway!" Mallory said suddenly, an idea popping into her head.

"What?" Woody turned his frightened face toward her.

"I'll go get my dollhouse father," Mallory told him, rising from the floor. "He has a nice little dark-blue suit made of felt and a lavender necktie," she added, as Woody closed his eyes and groaned.

"You wait here," she ordered. "I'll be right back."

The dollhouse was kept in the guest room because it took up too much space in Mallory's room. Mallory rushed upstairs and plucked Mr. Hemingway from his living room, where he was sitting stiffly on the couch beside Mrs. Hemingway, staring at a tiny TV set in the corner. The two Hemingway children were lying upstairs on their beds, where she and Alison had left them several days ago. Feverishly she stripped Mr. Hemingway of his coat, white shirt, necktie, and trousers and carried the clothes back downstairs.

"I'm sorry there're no shoes," she told Woody apologetically, "but Mr. Hemingway's are painted on his feet."

"Turn around," Woody ordered squeakily as she laid the clothes on the floor. Mallory sat down on a dining-room chair. In a moment Woody had dressed himself in Mr. Hemingway's suit, which fit surprisingly well. Mallory could only stare at him in dumb fascination. Alison's mother thought he was a "hunk"— Alison had told her so. But you certainly couldn't say that about him now!

"What can have happened to me?" Woody asked helplessly. "What can possibly have happened?"

"Maybe it was something you ate," Mallory suggested, though she couldn't imagine any food doing this to a person.

"Food doesn't make people shrink," Woody

said impatiently. "Besides, we've both just eaten the same things for supper." He turned a dazed look at the leg of the dining-room table rising above him like the trunk of a giant sequoia tree.

All at once Mallory thought about Mrs. Peebles and her shrunken cat. Could there possibly be any connection between Woody's condition and Alice's? Woody had eaten a butter cream and Mallory had had the penuche. But surely there was no way a candy could reduce someone's size; if anything, it would do the opposite. Still, the picture of little Alice curled up on the newspapers stayed in Mallory's mind. There was only one thing to do.

"I'm calling Mrs. Peebles," she announced. "She's the lady who made the candy you just ate."

"But what does she have to do with anything?" Woody asked, plowing laboriously after her through the high pile of the dining room carpet.

"I noticed today when I was at Becker's that

her cat had shrunk, and there just might be a connection."

"Oh yes, I'm sure Mrs. Peebles feeds her cat and her customers butter creams that make them into miniatures," Woody muttered.

In the kitchen Mallory had no difficulty finding Mrs. Peebles' number in the telephone directory in her mother's desk. There were just two Peebleses listed, Loretta M. at one number and Rudolph W. at the other. She dialed the first, and at the third ring a voice answered, "Loretta Peebles here."

"Mrs. Peebles, this is Mallory Watson," Mallory said. "We've got sort of a problem. My stepfather has just shrunk."

There was silence on the other end of the line. "No kidding," Mrs. Peebles said at last. "What, is he about the size of Alice?"

"Much, much smaller," Mallory told her. "I mean right now the only thing that fits him is my dollhouse father's suit."

"So we're talking really tiny," Mrs. Peebles murmured.

"I know how silly this sounds," Mallory said,

"but do you think it's possible one of your candies might have made my stepfather shrink?"

"Which candy did your stepdad eat?" Mrs. Peebles inquired in a tight voice.

"Woody ate the butter cream," Mallory said.

"Oh boy!"

"What?" Mallory asked apprehensively.

"I thought I'd thrown all those stupid diet candies away," Mrs. Peebles said. "I mean after what happened to Alice."

Mallory's eyes grew wide with alarm. "What diet candies?" she asked, not sure she wanted to hear the answer. She felt a tug on the telephone cord. "What's she saying?" Woody hissed.

"Well, it's Rudy's fault," Mrs. Peebles was saying defensively. "I never did trust that Lose It Now."

"Lose It Now?" Mallory repeated weakly.

"Oh, it's this compound Rudy came up with," Mrs. Peebles said. "I should have known better than to try it in my candy, and I didn't, not until four days ago anyway."

"'Can you imagine what a successful diet candy would do for us, Loretta?' Rudy said. 'We'd be on Easy Street for the rest of our lives.' He brought me over some Lose It Now in a plastic bag. It's this pink powder, and finally I decided to put the tiniest smidgen into some butter creams. But when I gave Alice one—I thought I should experiment on an animal first—and saw how small she got, naturally I wasn't going to try any out on humans."

"Well, how did Woody happen to get some, then?" Mallory demanded indignantly.

"Hard to say," Mrs. Peebles replied in a puzzled voice. "Like I said, I thought I'd dumped out my experimental batch, but somehow that one little piece with Rudy's compound must have gotten mixed in with the new batch. I sure am sorry about that, Mallory."

Now there was a very good chance, Mallory thought, that her mother would blame her for Woody's condition. Oh, if only she had not bought that candy!

"What is going on?" Woody demanded, trying to shinny up the leg of Mallory's chair. "Is that woman saying something about the candy?"

Mallory nodded, holding her hand over the receiver. "We may have to sue Mrs. Peebles," she whispered. Since Woody, who was a lawyer, had married her mother, Mallory had become very interested in words like *lawsuit* and *defendant* and *prosecutor.*

"Mallory, are you there?" Mrs. Peebles' voice asked.

Mallory turned back to the phone.

"What we've got to do is get in touch with Rudy to see if he knows how we can help poor Mr. Sherman," Mrs. Peebles said.

"Will you call him on the phone, right this very minute?" Mallory asked urgently. She looked down and saw that Woody was halfway up the chair leg.

"I want to talk to that woman," he insisted breathlessly.

"I don't know if she'll be able to hear you," Mallory said dubiously. She helped him up onto the desk and tried to position the receiver close to his head. "She says she's sure it was the butter cream that did this to you. It shrunk her cat, too."

"Oh, this gets better and better," Woody said, giving a bleak laugh as he attempted to lean into the mouthpiece. "Mrs. Peebles, what is going on here?" he cried. "I want an explanation at once."

"Mallory, are you still there?" Mallory could hear Mrs. Peebles' voice quite clearly. Gently she disengaged Woody's hands from the phone and held the receiver to her own ear.

"We got static on the phone or something," Mrs. Peebles said. "I was getting this squeaking noise for a minute there."

"That was Woody," Mallory told her. "You see, Mrs. Peebles, here's the thing. My mom is away, but she's coming home on Sunday. If she sees her new husband like this"—she glanced at Woody, who was leaning up against the pencil jar, staring moodily at the phone— "well, she's going to be really upset."

"I'll call Rudy at once and get right back to you," Mrs. Peebles said. "I just hope he's in town. He's gone back into show biz, you know."

"Show biz?" Mallory echoed.

"Oh, yes, he's a 1950 graduate of the Marvella Magicians' Institute, Northeastern Division," Mrs. Peebles said proudly. "For quite a few years there he did private parties, conventions, things like that. But he'd always been fascinated with science so he took some night courses at Jefferson Village Community College and went to work full-time as a lab technician at one of those big pharmaceutical plants out on Route 103. That's where he came up with his laundry soap and toothpaste. But show biz was still in his blood. Four months ago he joined a carnival as a magician. They've been touring the South, but they were due back in town yesterday. They're doing a show over in Wildwood this weekend."

"Call him," Mallory begged.

"Sure thing," Mrs. Peebles agreed. "Try not to fret too much now. Rudy usually comes through in a pinch. He's a little weird, I'll have to admit, but basically he has a good heart."

"Mallory, will you tell me what's happening?" Woody asked in an anguished voice as Mallory hung up the phone.

"Mr. Peebles is the one who invented this ingredient that Mrs. Peebles put in her candy," Mallory explained. "It was supposed to help people lose weight but when it shrank her cat, Mrs. Peebles threw it all away except for that piece you got by mistake. She's calling Mr. Peebles right away to tell him what's happened."

Woody rolled his eyes at the ceiling. "I've wandered into a lair of loonies," he said, shaking his head. He turned his gaze on Mallory. "You know, lots of people think New York City is a dangerous place with the robberies and the muggings and everything. Well, it's nothing compared to what goes on in Jefferson Village, believe me."

"I'm sorry," Mallory apologized. She almost added, "I wish it had been me who ate that candy," but she didn't. She couldn't really wish that such a dreadful thing would happen to her.

"I realized the minute you rode off on your bike this afternoon that your mom wouldn't have let you go into town if she'd been here," Woody said. "In fact, I even started down the street after you, but you'd already turned the corner. Now see what's happened?" He gave her an accusing look that made Mallory feel like a criminal. And why shouldn't she feel that way? If she had just followed her mother's orders and stayed at home, none of this would have happened.

They both jumped as the telephone rang.

"Mrs. Peebles," Mallory began as she grabbed the receiver; however, it was her mother calling to say she had arrived safely at Aunt Karen's.

"The baby is simply adorable," Mrs. Sherman gushed. "You're going to just love him, Mal." And then she asked, trying, Mallory thought, to sound nonchalant, "You and Woody doing okay?"

"It's Mom," Mallory whispered to her step-father.

"Can I speak to Woody?" Mrs. Sherman asked.

"He's, er, in the shower right now," Mallory said, looking at Woody, who nodded approval of her fib.

"Well, tell him I called and that I'll be home sometime in the early afternoon on Sunday."

As she hung up, Mallory tried to do a rapid calculation of how much time she and Woody had before her mother's return. She couldn't come up with the exact number of hours in her head; all she knew was that there weren't nearly enough of them. She began to chew nervously at the end of her ponytail as she stared at the phone, willing Mrs. Peebles to call back.

"Why aren't we hearing from that woman?" Woody asked a minute or two later. He was sitting cross-legged on top of the desk. Now he got up and began pacing restlessly. And then a second later the phone did ring.

"Hello, hon, it's just me again," Mrs. Peebles said when Mallory picked up the receiver. "I called Rudy and got his answering machine. I left a message for him to call me the minute he gets in. I guess we're just going to have to sit tight until we hear from him."

"Mr. Peebles isn't at home," Mallory told Woody, who had stopped his pacing to come stand at her elbow. She turned her attention back to the phone. "Will you call us the minute you hear from him?" she begged Mrs. Peebles, "no matter what time it is?"

"You bet," Mrs. Peebles promised. "Now try to take it easy, and if I were you I'd keep the little fella warm. A teeny guy like that, no flesh on his bones, could catch cold very easily."

Mallory placed the phone back in its cradle and looked distractedly at her watch. She saw that it was almost time for *Crime Time*, another show her mother disapproved of. However, Woody happened to like it too, and her mother was always pleased to see them enjoying the same thing, even if it was a cops-and-robbers drama. She usually made a bowl of popcorn for them to nibble on while they watched.

"*Crime Time* will be on in another minute," she said, putting out her hand to scoop Woody up. But he shied away from her.

"I don't like being carted around, Mallory," he said testily. "I'm not a toy, you know. Just help me off the desk. I can get into the den under my own steam."

"Okay," Mallory said, reminding herself that no matter how small he had become, Woody still needed to be treated with respect. She walked slowly down the hall in order to give him a chance to catch up with her. But no matter how she dawdled, he was still barely in sight by the time she reached the den. The first set of commercials was over by the time he made it to the couch, huffing from exertion. She restrained herself from lifting him up beside her and pretended she saw nothing unusual in his sitting on the floor, his back propped against the leg of the coffee table.

Woody couldn't concentrate on *Crime Time* any more than she could. He got up and paced. He asked Mallory for the time every few minutes; then he stretched out on his back on the floor with his hands over his eyes. She was very worried about him.

Just before the end of the show she had an inspiration. "Woody, I have a good idea about where you can sleep tonight," she said.

"Where?" he asked uninterestedly, staring up at the ceiling from his prone position on the floor.

"In the dollhouse," Mallory told him.

Woody gave her an offended look. "Thanks for the suggestion," he said, "but I see no reason why I shouldn't sleep in my own room."

Yet later, when they went upstairs, with Mallory carrying him carefully in one hand because the height of the stair treads had proved too much for him, he did look terribly lost in the king-size bed he and her mother shared.

"Just let me look the dollhouse over," he requested grudgingly. Mallory carried him into the guest room and set him down in the fancy blue bedroom on the second floor.

"See, Grandma made a spread for the bed." She pointed to the blue-and-white-striped comforter about the size of a single patch in a patchwork quilt.

"I suppose I should settle in here," Woody said with a sigh.

"I think you'll be very comfortable," Mallory said encouragingly. "I'll leave a light on for you." The dollhouse was electrified and had lights in almost every room. She snapped on the one in the hall.

"Thanks," Woody said. He sat down on the edge of the bed, testing the mattress. He looked up at Mallory. "There's a chance I might grow back to normal, you know," he said, trying to sound optimistic. "I mean, there's no reason to think this condition is permanent."

"That's right," Mallory agreed quickly, relieved that he was at least trying to take a more positive outlook. But as she made her way to her own room, she felt very doubtful about the possibility of a growth spurt for Woody. And what if he did grow a little—but only to about the size of a first grader? Or what if he grew lopsidedly, she fretted, as she got into her pajamas. His head might grow to its normal size but his arms and legs might remain tiny and spindly.

"It's not going to be a very good night for sleeping," she predicted, turning the covers down on her bed. "Not a good night at all."

3

The Break-In

MALLORY SLEPT FITFULLY once she managed to doze off, but sometime in the middle of the night she awoke with a start. She had heard a muffled thump somewhere, she was sure. Could Woody have gone downstairs for some reason? She lay perfectly still, hardly daring to breathe, feeling peculiarly alone. Of course she wasn't really, but with Woody so small, it almost seemed that way. She strained her ears, but the house remained silent. The grandfather clock in the hall quietly struck two. Mallory relaxed a little at the comfortingly familiar sound and closed her eyes. A second later they flew open again as that floorboard between the dining room and the hall gave its familiar creak. There was someone downstairs!

She sat straight up in her bed. She wasn't going to lie there and wait for some stranger to come sidling up the stairs—that was for sure. She eased herself out of bed and picked up her tennis racket, which was lying on a chair next to the door. She crept from the room. In the hall below she could see the tall clock. It was standing like a sentry in the moonlight that streamed in from the glass panels on either side of the front door. Halfway down the stairs she was also able to make out a man in jeans and a jeans jacket opening the drawer in the hall table. In one hand he held a flashlight. At his feet was a large canvas bag. Her heart lurched with fear.

Why had she ever imagined she'd be able to frighten off this burglar with a tennis racket? As she was thinking seriously of backing her way upstairs, the man, perhaps sensing the presence of someone else in the room, suddenly wheeled and looked straight at Mallory. She stared at him, shivering in her pajamas and bare feet. For a moment she thought he had no face at all. Then she realized he was wearing a ski mask. He moved swiftly to the bottom of the stairs, never taking his eyes off her.

"Come down here," he said, beckoning with his finger. He spoke softly, but Mallory could tell he meant business. She hesitated.

"Now," said the man. As though in a trance she moved toward him. He reached out and clamped a hand around her wrist.

"If you'd rather not have your teeth shoved down your throat, keep quiet, understand?" he said. Mallory winced and nodded. She wondered what he meant to steal; from the looks of his sack he had gotten hold of the silver already. He probably had thought no one was at home, with her mother's station wagon gone and Woody's car down at Nelson's Garage for a tune-up. Then she remembered with a stab of horror it had been up to her to lock the house at bedtime, which of course had never occurred to her. She had made it easy for the burglar. He'd simply been able to stroll right into the kitchen through the garage.

He looked past her at the stairs, regretting perhaps that he couldn't go up to the second floor now that he realized the house was not empty after all.

Suddenly he tensed and stepped backward, dragging Mallory with him. In the moonlight she saw something that looked like a little dark starfish somersaulting down the stairs and landing cleverly on its feet in the hallway.

"Let go of her, you creep!" Woody ordered, his voice cracking with the strain of trying to shout. "Or I'll turn you into a mini midget. In fact, I may anyway." He stepped menacingly toward the burglar, who had directed the beam of his flashlight on the strange creature before him.

"What the ___ is that?" The burglar ut-
tered a word that Mallory's mother had yelled
at her for using.

"I mean what I say," Woody repeated. "I like
turning people into mini midgets. I do it fre-
quently. You've got five seconds to let go of
that girl and get out of here, six at the most."

"Who the ___ is that?" Mallory could hear
the fear in his voice, feel it in the way his
hand tightened painfully on her wrist. And
she suddenly had an idea.

"Oh boy, it's one of them," she muttered,
shaking her head.

"One of who?" the burglar asked warily,
squeezing her wrist so tightly she almost cried
out.

"One of the little people who live in this
house," she whispered.

"You're crazy," the burglar said huskily.
"You're off your spool."

"The thing is not to make them mad," Mallory said in a low voice. "That's when they
spit out the poison."

"I've been working too hard, that's it, I've

been driving myself," the burglar muttered, suddenly letting go of Mallory to try to wipe the sweat from his upper lip without removing his ski mask. From the corner of her eye, Mallory observed Woody creeping off toward the burglar's sack. What was he up to? Why didn't he help her by speaking up, adding a little something about the poison spit she'd thought of?

"They're always worse, the LPs—that's what we call them—when the moon is full," Mallory said, sweating herself.

"I'm outta here," the burglar mumbled. He stepped toward his sack, and as he bent to pick it up, from out of the top flashed something that looked like a little dagger. The burglar let out a bleat and drew his hand back.

"There's another one in there!" he cried. "He cut me—I'm bleeding!" Mallory had never seen anyone take off faster than the burglar as he made a dash for the kitchen door. On top of his abandoned sack stood Woody, fiercely brandishing one of her mother's silver-handled steak knives.

"Is he gone?" he asked cautiously, lowering the knife to knee level. Mallory, straining her ears, did think she heard the faint sound of running feet slapping down the driveway.

"Oh wow!" she said, feeling her legs go all wobbly. Woody jumped down from the sack and joined her on the bottom step of the stairs.

"You were terrific," he told her admiringly. "It's gonna be some time before that guy has the guts to sneak into a dark house again."

"It was very brave of you to come down the stairs like that," Mallory told him breathily, "but we were lucky the burglar didn't just laugh at you." The intruder could have done worse than laughed, she thought with a shudder. He could easily have picked Woody up and squished him between his fingers like a bug.

"Well, when you're a lawyer, sometimes you have to do a little bluffing," Woody said. He looked closely at her. "You're okay?" he asked. "That jerk didn't hurt you?"

Mallory shook her head and they sat in

silence for a while, trying to pull themselves together. Finally Mallory got up, switched on the hall light, and looked in the burglar's sack. She saw her mother's silver biscuit box gleaming inside. She pulled it out and set it on the hall table. Then she took out handfuls of knives and forks and spoons and a silver bowl that had belonged to her great-aunt.

"I'll put these things away tomorrow," she said, suddenly overwhelmed by fatigue. She looked at Woody. "Did you really cut the burglar?" she asked.

"Just nicked his thumb," he replied. He blew out a tiny puff of air between his lips. "If anyone had ever told me I'd have a night like this, I would have laughed in that person's face," he said.

"Tomorrow things are bound to get better," Mallory said, though she wasn't at all sure they would. "I'll help you back to bed, but first I'm going to lock the back door. We don't want any more surprise visitors, ever."

"The next one might not be such a dim bulb," Woody agreed.

4

A Visit to Rudy Peebles'

WHEN MALLORY AWOKE the next morning, her first conscious thought was of Woody. She jumped out of bed and hurried into the hall, half expecting to see him in her mother's room, normal in every way. All the awful things that had happened last night, seen in the clear light of this beautiful spring day, would be no more than a bad dream. But when she went into the guest room, there he was, standing at the front door of the dollhouse. He was staring moodily off across the expanse of pink shag carpet. And he was still only three inches tall.

"I was hoping you might have grown in the night," she said, "even just a little." Her gaze traveled beyond him to the dollhouse kitchen. On the floor was one of the cups from the tiny set of dishes that filled the cupboard over the sink.

"Where did that come from?" she asked, not remembering having seen the cup there yesterday. Woody looked embarrassed. "Dollhouse bathrooms aren't exactly functional, if you know what I mean," he explained. "The john, well, it's just made of plastic and the lid doesn't come up or anything. The cup was the best I could come up with."

"Oh well, it's not a problem," Mallory said, trying to sound casual. She crossed the room and as discreetly as possible, reached into the kitchen. As she was about to lift the little cup in her hand, the doorbell rang downstairs.

"Who can that be?" she said in alarm.

"What time is it?" Woody asked, making no protest as she assisted him from the dollhouse.

"Eight-fifteen," she said in surprise. "I didn't know I'd slept so late. What should I do about the door?"

"You'd better see who's there," Woody advised as the bell pealed again. "If it's a neighbor, tell them I'm shaving."

Foreseeing a long weekend of fibs and excuses, Mallory hurried downstairs, absentmindedly carrying Woody in her hand. Not knowing exactly what to do with him, she dropped him in the china bowl on the hall table.

"Mallory!" he objected in an indignant voice as she opened the front door.

There on the steps stood Mrs. Peebles, clad in a bright-blue polyester pantsuit.

"How's Mr. Sherman this morning?" she inquired, lowering her voice. "Grown a little since last night, has he?"

"Not even a fraction of an inch," Mallory reported, standing aside to let Mrs. Peebles enter.

"Alice showed a little growth spurt after taking Rudy's compound," Mrs. Peebles said, "but animals don't always react like humans, I guess. Besides, I gave her the compound mixed in a bowl of Kitty Kibbles, not in a piece of candy. That might explain the difference, too. Where is Mr. Sherman? I'm dying to see him."

"Over there," Mallory said unhappily, pointing behind her.

Mrs. Peebles turned her eyes in the direction of the china bowl. "Oh, my word!" she said, raising the eyeglasses attached to a cord around her neck. "Can I pick him up?"

"You certainly cannot," Woody said. "Mallory, will you get me out of this thing?"

Mallory lifted him from the bowl and placed him on the table beside it.

"Where is your husband?" he demanded of Mrs. Peebles.

"Well, I can't just say," she replied, her eyes

riveted to Woody's tiny frame. "I tried to reach him five or six times last night and just kept getting his answering machine. I haven't phoned yet today. Rudy sleeps in on Saturday mornings, and he gets very cranky if you wake him."

"Mrs. Peebles, look at me. Can't you see what's happened?" Woody asked, slowly circling the top of the hall table. "Do you really think, under the circumstances, that I care about Mr. Peebles being disturbed?"

"I'm sure you don't," Mrs. Peebles said soothingly. "What I think we should do is—"

"I simply can't understand how Mr. Peebles could have come up with a—a shrinking powder," Woody said. "Is he a sorcerer or what?"

"Well, he has a little laboratory down in his basement all full of test tubes and beakers and stuff. Fascinating place. Now, I was about to say I think we should all drive over together to Rudy's to see if he's at home. He's not always good about answering his telephone messages."

"Just let me get dressed," Mallory said, and

flew upstairs, leaving Woody in the hall. In her room she grabbed whatever she could find and reappeared three minutes later clad in a red, not-too-clean T-shirt and pink shorts and sneakers without socks. She fetched a doughnut from the kitchen. With the doughnut in one hand and Woody in the other, she followed Mrs. Peebles out to her big blue car parked in the driveway. Both front fenders were dented, and it was easy to see why once they got under way. Mrs. Peebles was rather an absentminded driver, drifting from time to time so close to the curb that Mallory held her breath, expecting to feel the right front tire scrape up against it at any moment. At traffic lights, if engrossed in conversation, she came to halts so abruptly that Mallory had to grab hold of Woody, who was standing on the seat beside her.

It was a great relief finally to arrive at Mr. Peebles' house on a little street on the outskirts of town. Brushing doughnut crumbs from her lap, she picked Woody up and followed Mrs. Peebles from the car and up the front walk, taking note of the yard and the lawn figure of a gnome in the middle of it. Mrs. Peebles rang the bell and, when there was no answer, rang it again. She pressed her face to one of the glass panels that flanked the front door.

"House looks deserted," she reported. "Maybe Herman can help us out."

"Herman?" Mallory waited for further explanation.

"Him." Mrs. Peebles nodded at the gnome on the front lawn.

"Do you get the feeling we are about to view another of Mr. Peebles' marvels?" Woody grumbled as Mallory plodded across the lawn after Mrs. Peebles.

"No, Herman was mostly Randall's idea," Mrs. Peebles said. "Randall is Rudy's younger brother."

"Got anything for me, Herman?" she asked, looking into the gnome's roguish plaster face. And then she reached under his beard and pushed a button. Herman's mouth fell open and slowly, like a protruding tongue, a wide ribbon of white paper appeared. Mrs. Peebles tore it off at the perforation just before Herman's jaw snapped shut.

"Rudy often leaves messages for me," she explained, looking sternly at Mallory and Woody as though she thought they might not believe her.

"I mean Rudy and I still keep in touch, even though he's living here and I'm over in the Elmcrest condos."

She put on her glasses and read aloud what Herman had printed out: "Loretta, as you know, the carnival opens Saturday night. I hope you'll stop by to say hello. Anytime after eight will be fine."

Mrs. Peebles folded the note and put it in the pocket of her pantsuit.

"Well that works out pretty well then," she said with satisfaction. "I can pick you both up at, let's see, about seven-thirty. Will that be okay?"

"Oh gosh, that's such a long time to wait." Mallory sighed, looking at her wristwatch.

"I think it's the best we can do," Mrs.

Peebles said, turning toward the car. "And of course there's always the chance that Mr. Sherman will have a growth spurt during the day."

"If you believe that, you'll believe anything," Woody said glumly.

"Well, if you don't grow . . . " Mrs. Peebles opened the door on the driver's side and slid, with a grunt, behind the wheel. "Phew, it's going to be a hot one today," she predicted.

"If I don't grow, what?" Woody asked as Mallory got into the passenger seat.

"You could make a fortune going on tour," Mrs. Peebles pointed out, turning on the ignition. "Folks would pay big money to see the world's tiniest man." Warming to the subject, she continued, "I could be your manager, maybe. Through my sister, the gal who's on the soap, I've met some show business types who—" She broke off as she caught a glimpse of Woody's face.

"Oh, well, it was just an idea," she said quickly, and turned her attention to the road.

5

The Kidnapping

THE DAY LOOMED endlessly ahead after Mrs. Peebles dropped Mallory and Woody off in their driveway. She promised to pick them up that evening.

"I think I'll go see how my plants are doing," Woody said with a sigh. "I can't just sit around the house all day."

He had put in some zinnia and snapdragon

slips two weeks before. Every evening after work he went out to inspect them in the back-yard.

"I'll go with you," Mallory said at once. "You might get lost or something."

"No, I can handle this myself," he told her firmly. But Mallory insisted on accompanying him. He would not, however, allow her to carry him across the kitchen nor down the three steps that led from the back door out to the backyard. These he handled quite skill-fully, leaping from one to the other.

"My plants have really grown," he said in awe when they reached the garden. Actually they hadn't grown that much, Mallory ob-served, but at Woody's present size, the small plants must have looked like a cornfield to him.

"It'll be nice when they get buds and begin to bloom," she said encouragingly but then fell silent. She had the awful feeling that when that happened, Woody might possibly be no bigger than he was now. She just didn't dare think about the future.

At eleven o'clock a girl named Meegan Phillips called to ask Mallory over for lunch.

"Go," Woody signaled at her as she hesitated, the telephone in her hand. "I'll be all right."

It wasn't just concern for Woody that made Mallory waver. Meegan Phillips was not a close friend, and while she could be fun, she could also be a real goofball. Two weeks ago in school she had been doing a mock ballet dance in the hall and her shoe had flown off, shattering the glass on a picture of a sixth-grade class taken in 1972. For that she had been sent to the principal's office.

However, with Woody's urging, Mallory decided maybe it would help pass the time if she were to get out of the house for a while.

"You've been good to me, Mallory, since my, er, problem," Woody told her gravely. "Go and try to have some fun."

So Mallory went, hoping that Meegan's mother might have baked a cake that morning. She put a blueberry on a dollhouse plate for Woody and poured a few drops of milk into a tiny goblet, one of a set of six her grandmother had sent. She left his lunch on the coffee table in the den and turned the TV on for him.

"You're sure you're gonna be all right?" she asked, watching him shinny up the slipcover onto the seat of the sofa.

"Don't worry, I can take care of myself," he assured her.

"I won't be gone long," she promised, and left the house, feeling guilty and entirely unsure that leaving him alone was the right thing to do.

Meegan's mother served chicken salad sandwiches and, for dessert, delicious lemon bars. But for the first time in her life, Mallory found she had no appetite. She was too nervous about things at home to enjoy food, even Mrs. Phillips'.

"You eat like a bird," Meegan's mother told her. "Here, I'll wrap up a lemon bar for you to take home."

After lunch Mallory and Meegan went into the playroom. Meegan had several stuffed horses with whom they acted out stories. Mallory liked the love story they thought up for two of the horses, but after a while Meegan grew bored and began acting up, throwing the horses in the air and overturning the stables Mallory had made from some cardboard cartons.

"The horses look grubby," Meegan announced suddenly, and gathering up her own horse and Mallory's, she carried them into the bathroom. Wondering how Woody was doing home alone, Mallory watched Meegan fill the tub with water. Then Meegan added seven or eight generous dashes of bubble bath. The horses' manes and tails soon glistened with bubbles.

Just as Mallory was beginning to enjoy shampooing her horse, Meegan said: "Let's pretend my guy is the Horse King of the Sea and decides to stir up a big storm." She began swishing her animal through the water and making bigger and bigger waves, soaking the front of Mallory's shirt with one particularly large breaker.

Enough is enough, Mallory thought, and rose from the bath mat on which she had been kneeling.

"I've got to go," she declared, and though Meegan coaxed her to stay, she thanked Mrs. Phillips for the lunch and hurried determinedly toward home.

The house was very quiet when she got home. The TV was still on, but Woody was nowhere in sight. Mallory made a quick tour of the downstairs, then, thinking that perhaps he was napping, went upstairs to check the dollhouse. There was no sign of him. He was not in her mother's room or her own room or the bathroom.

"Woody!" she called, growing more anxious by the moment. She ran downstairs, rechecking each room again, calling his name. No answer.

"Can he have gone outside again?" she asked herself, trying to stay calm. She went out the kitchen door and circled the backyard, softly calling his name as she went.

"I'm looking for Woody too," a man's voice

said. From behind a stand of forsythia Mallory's next-door neighbor, Mr. Meres, appeared with a rake in his hand.

"I mentioned that I'd bring over the screws he needs to put that exercise bar of yours up in the doorway of your room." Mr. Meres looked at her curiously. "You over here alone?"

"No, Woody had to run to the store," Mallory said quickly. "I thought maybe he'd gotten back already. He'll probably be home soon."

"Well, tell him I've got his screws," Mr. Meres said.

Mallory thanked him and walked around the side of the house. She was touched to learn that Woody had intended to put up the exercise bar she had bought with the money she'd earned herself. Of course Woody was not too swift with a screwdriver, but still, he'd wanted to help.

All the times she had wished for him to get lost, she thought, pausing to part the branches of a hydrangea bush, and now that he actually was, she was in a panic.

"Woody, can you hear me?" she called loudly over the sound of Mr. Meres' lawn mower. How long should she search for him on her own, she wondered, wishing there were someone here to help her. But if she were to telephone the police for assistance, she would have to describe her stepfather. Who was going to believe her when she said Woody was only about three inches tall?

She plodded across the front lawn, keeping her head bent so as not to step on him if he suddenly appeared beneath her feet.

When she had combed every inch of grass, she walked down the driveway, past the maple tree, past another clump of forsythia, past the white dogwood at the edge of the lawn. She moved slowly down one side of Pilgrim Road and then up the other without meeting anyone. Everyone was out doing errands or having fun, like normal families.

Am I going to have to tell Mom I lost Woody? she wondered, trudging back along her driveway. I can say he just disappeared without ever having to tell her about the shrinkage, she thought, sitting down heavily on the front steps. But no, of course she would have to tell her mother everything. She glanced at her watch. Four-thirty. Should she call Mrs. Peebles and let her know what had happened? What would that accomplish, though? There was nothing Mrs. Peebles could do. Yet she had a desperate need to talk to someone about this emergency. All at once she thought of her father. Even though he was fifty miles away in New York City, he might be able to give her some good advice.

She went into the kitchen and dialed his number. She pictured the telephone on the kitchen wall of his apartment ringing into an empty room. The phone rang five or six times; just as she was ready to hang up, her father answered. He sounded as he so often did, as though he had just arrived home, or was already there but was in a hurry to go out again.

"Dad, it's me," Mallory said, relieved to hear his voice.

"Mal, what a nice surprise!" he said, sounding genuinely glad to hear from her. "I'm just off to tennis. That new indoor center I told you about opened last week. I have a doubles game in about twenty minutes."

Mallory hesitated. She ought to quickly tell him about Woody, but somehow explaining the shrinking and then Woody's disappearance seemed too much to squeeze into a two-minute conversation.

"I just wondered how you were," she said lamely.

"I'm fine, sweetheart," he said cheerily, "and I'm looking forward to our date in a couple of weeks. I've got the circus tickets tucked away in my bureau drawer."

"That's good, Dad," Mallory said, trying to sound enthusiastic.

"Say hello to Mom and Woody for me," her father said. "I've got to run. I'll talk to you soon." And that was that. Really, what could he have done to help out with a problem as bizarre as hers? She hung the phone back in its cradle, deciding she'd take one more look for Woody in the backyard.

She was standing under the big pine tree when she heard it: a tiny, familiar voice calling her name from a spot high above her head. Her glance shot upward.

"Mallory!" the voice called again. "Help me!"

"Woody, is that you?" Mallory's heart leaped with hope. Shading her eyes from the late afternoon sun, she squinted up through the pine branches. At the very top of the tree she could make out a large, untidy-looking nest. And was that a tiny head sticking out from the top?

"Woody, how in the world did you get up there?" Mallory cried, relief flooding over her. But in the next moment the question of how to get him down presented itself.

"I'm going to have to jump," he called to her. "You'll have to get a blanket or something and try to hold it out for me to land in."

I don't know how I can hold a blanket without someone to help me, Mallory thought. But then she had an idea.

"I'll be right back," she called, cupping her mouth with her hands. "Hang in there, Woody."

She ran to the garage and grabbed her butterfly net, which was propped up against the wall.

"Do you think you can manage to jump into this?" she asked, arriving breathlessly back at the tree.

"It's not very big," Woody said doubtfully, hanging over the edge of the nest, "but I've got to get out of here before that crow returns."

Mallory positioned herself close to the trunk of the pine and held the net out in front of her with both hands. She watched nervously as Woody climbed onto the rim of the nest. She thought she heard him counting to three. Bravely he leaped off into space, hurtling toward her much faster than she expected. He let out a grunt as she caught him in the center of the net, where, like an acrobat on a trampoline, he bounced upward twice, appearing to be very much in control. But then he fell onto his back and lay in the net without moving.

"Woody, please be okay," Mallory pleaded, looking at the still figure. She plucked him out of the net and peered intently into his face. It was very pale and she couldn't tell if he was breathing or not. What to do now? Even if she knew CPR, could it be performed on anyone so small? She loosened his tie and, as gently as though he were a butterfly, carried him into the house with the intention of trying to revive him with a drop or two of water. But as she turned on the tap in the kitchen, he stirred in her hand.

"Where am I?" he asked groggily, struggling to sit up.

"You're safe now," Mallory said, setting him on the counter. "How did you ever get up in that tree, Woody?"

"It was terrible," he said, looking gratefully around the kitchen. "I may never leave the house again. It's too dangerous out there."

Mallory waited quietly for him to go on.

"Well, I decided to go for a little stroll around the property while you were at your friend's," he told her, "even though it was difficult to see much in that thick grass. I don't know who's going to mow it for me now," he worried. "I promised your mother I'd get it done while she was gone."

Long grass is going to be the least of her problems when she gets home, Mallory thought with apprehension.

"I was looking up at the sky," he said, "thinking how only a few days ago I was in a plane, flying to Chicago to see one of our clients. You know, the flight goes practically over our house and I remember looking out of the plane window, thinking about you and Mom down beneath the clouds and I was glad you were both there for me. While I was thinking that, this huge black winged thing, looking like something out of a creature feature movie, came flapping down, and the next thing I knew he had grabbed me by the seat of the pants in this beak of his. My lord, it looked like a dagger, and the creature was carrying me up in the air. I didn't know whether to struggle so he'd drop me or hold perfectly still so he wouldn't."

"I knew I should never have left you," Mallory groaned, thinking that while Woody was being taken captive, she was five blocks away, pretending two dumb stuffed horses were falling in love.

"For some reason we keep getting involved with thieves," Woody said, running his hand through his hair. "This crow that snatched me? His nest up there in the pine had all sorts of stuff in it that he'd obviously snitched—a blue bead, a dog tag, a piece of ribbon, and a maraschino cherry."

"Weird," Mallory said.

"And a bird's nest is not a great thing to sit in," he told her. "The twigs are held together with, I don't know, dried mud, bird poop, who knows."

"But that crow didn't try to peck you or anything, did he?" Mallory asked.

Woody shook his head. "He just looked at me with those bright inquisitive eyes of his and made this funny clicking noise in his throat and flew off. For a moment there I thought about trying to climb down to the ground, but I knew the branches were too far apart for me. When I heard you calling my name, I tried to shout at you, but Norm Meres' lawn mower was making such a racket, you couldn't hear me.

"I hate that pine tree," Woody said balefully. "I wish I'd had it cut down when Elmford Tree Service came around in April."

"They wanted too much money for the job," Mallory reminded him.

"I know," Woody said impatiently, "but if I'd realized I was going to be kidnapped by the crow thief who lived in it, I would have hired them anyway.

"I have a headache," he said suddenly.

"It's probably all the excitement," Mallory said. "Maybe you'd like to take a little rest."

"Not in the dollhouse. I don't like it there."

"How about the couch in the den?" Mallory suggested. "There must be a baseball game on TV—there always is."

"Would you watch with me for a little while?" he asked. "I don't feel like being alone."

"Sure," she said. "Let me get you down from the counter."

"Mal, wait," he said as she started to scoop him up. She paused, resting her hands on the edge of the counter.

"Thanks for coming to my rescue."

"Oh gosh, I'm just glad I found you," she said. He still looked pale and very rumpled and disheartened, and she wished there were something she could do to make him feel better.

"It's so undignified being this way," he said sadly, "and to you I'm some sort of nerd anyway. I can only imagine what you think of me now."

"Well, so I was wrong, you're not a nerd," Mallory said staunchly. "I think you're a very brave person."

"Really?" He looked at her uncertainly.

"I mean, it's just that you've always lived in the city," she tried to explain, "and you don't—I mean—you're not quite like—well, see, I never really expected Mom to get married again."

"I know," he said sympathetically.

She gave him a thoughtful look. "It's probably not easy trying to learn how to be a stepfather," she said.

"Boy, you can say that again." Woody rolled his eyes toward the ceiling.

Funny, Mallory thought, it had never occurred to her that he might be having as much of a problem getting used to her as she was getting used to him.

"Maybe I would have done better with a stepson," he said thoughtfully.

"What, are you kidding me?" Mallory cried. "Who would ever want a nine-year-old stepson? Ugh!" And she clutched at her throat as though the very thought made her feel sick.

Woody gave her a wan smile. "Mal, do you realize we're actually talking to each other, having a real conversation?"

"Well," Mallory said slowly, "we should have more of them." And she decided then and there that if they could just get Woody back to normal, she would invite him to the father-daughter dinner her Girl Scout troop was having in June. Up till now, she'd been pretty hard on him; maybe he needed a little sympathy.

"Let's go watch TV," she said. "I think the Cleveland Indians are playing." Actually she had heard the team's name mentioned on the TV at Meegan's. Mr. and Mrs. Phillips, both avid baseball fans, had been watching the game together after lunch.

"One of the best players for the Indians is this rookie named Fernando Sanchez," she continued, reporting what she thought she had heard the television sportscaster saying. "He's a free swinger, but that's okay because he almost always makes contact." Mallory thought, let any stepson come up with more authoritative information than that!

"Sanchez is a good player," Woody agreed, smiling. "The only thing is, he plays for the Yankees."

"Oh," Mallory said. "Well, whatever," and picked her stepfather up expertly between her thumb and forefinger and carried him to the den.

6

Search and Rescue

MRS. PEEBLES, true to her promise, arrived promptly at seven-thirty. She was dressed in another pantsuit, this one bright red. Her dangling earrings were fake rubies.

Mallory had decided to wear her new pink jumper because of the two big pockets in the skirt.

"Now I know how a joey must feel," Woody mumbled from the depths of the left-hand pocket.

"What's a joey?" she asked, opening the door of Mrs. Peebles' car.

"A baby kangaroo," he explained.

"I still think we're missing the boat here, not taking the little fella on tour," Mrs. Peebles whispered as she slid behind the driver's seat.

"I heard that," Woody said from the pocket, "and I hope for the last time."

"Whatever you say, Mr. Sherman," Mrs. Peebles said, sailing blithely out of Pilgrim Road. "You're the boss." She glared indignantly at a driver who had blown his horn at her for pulling out in front of him. "What's that turkey honking for?" she said. "People are so impatient these days."

The trip to Wildwood took twenty minutes. The carnival's dusty parking lot was almost filled when they pulled into it. Mrs. Peebles remarked cheerfully that Mallory would have to remember where they left the car because she herself was very bad at recalling things like that.

Mallory raised her eyes to the lazily revolving arc of the Ferris wheel, glittering in the twilight. She loved Ferris wheels, but tonight she had more important things on her mind. Even the enticing smell of sizzling hot dogs from across the parking lot could not distract her from the business of locating Mr. Peebles.

"Does your husband have his own booth or is he in a tent?" Mallory asked as they passed through the entrance gates.

"Good question," Mrs. Peebles said, turning briskly down the midway. She paused for a moment in front of a booth. It was lined with shelves of gifts that could be won by pricking one of the balloons tied to a dart board beneath them. "I have no idea where we'll find Rudy. We'll just have to keep our eyes peeled.

"Don't worry," she said, looking at Mallory's anxious face, "he'll turn up. He always does. How about some cotton candy? My treat."

Mallory hesitated. It seemed frivolous to be thinking of food at a time like this, but she did love cotton candy, so she gave in.

As they crossed the midway, Woody's head appeared above the rim of her pocket. "What does Peebles look like?" he inquired.

"Small, dark fella," Mrs. Peebles told him, taking her wallet from her purse. "Full head of curly dark hair. Good-looking. You should see him in a tux.

"Two, please," she said to the white-capped attendant who was deftly wrapping spun sugar around paper cones for a mother and daughter. "You can have a teeny bit of mine, Mr. Sherman," she whispered behind her hand to Woody as his head disappeared into the pocket.

They walked on. Mallory snapped distractedly at her cotton candy, pausing with Mrs. Peebles to look first at the Tilt-A-Whirl and then at the duck-shooting gallery, where a parade of little wooden ducks circled past on a conveyor belt.

"I'm suffocating down here," Woody complained. "I should have left my jacket at home. Mallory, can you help me take—"

"Hey, Mal, what's that big green stain on the back of your dress?" a voice said.

Mallory twirled around in consternation,

gathering up the hem of her skirt with one hand in an attempt to examine the fabric. And then the minute she saw that terrible dweeb from her class, Jerry Doolittle, grinning at her, she knew the stain was just his idea of a joke.

Irritated that she had fallen for the hoax, she gave him a bored look and said, "Boy, are you funny. I mean I'm really doubled up laughing."

Smoothing her skirt into place, she turned her back on him and concentrated on the business at hand.

"Mrs. Peebles," she asked worriedly, "can't we ask someone where your husband is?" Ever since entering the fairgrounds, she'd had this nagging doubt that perhaps Mr. Peebles was, for some reason, not at the carnival after all.

"Wouldn't hurt to ask George Tucci, I guess," Mrs. Peebles said. "He's a fella Rudy and I have known for years. Operates the merry-go-round now."

Even though their mission was urgent, Mallory had to take a few moments out from worrying to admire the horses on Mr. Tucci's carousel. They were stationary on the platform as she and Mrs. Peebles approached, jewels glinting in their saddles, their prancing hooves poised, waiting for the next riders to mount them. George Tucci, a short, heavy-set man wearing a red plaid shirt, waved at Mrs. Peebles from the well in the middle of the merry-go-round. "How's it going, Loretta?" he called. "Long time no see."

"I'm looking for Rudy," Mrs. Peebles said. "Any idea where he might be, George?"

"He said something earlier, when we were setting up, about getting a booth over by the fortune-teller's tent," Mr. Tucci told her. "Tell him I'll have a cup of coffee with him later if you see him."

Mrs. Peebles thanked Mr. Tucci and she and Mallory plodded back across the midway. It was then that Mallory reached into her pocket to check on Woody and her fingers closed on air. In disbelief she looked into the pocket, groping into the corners. She checked her other pocket. Both were empty.

"Mrs. Peebles, he's gone," she gasped. "I

can't find my stepfather!"

"Oh for pity's sake!" Mrs. Peebles stopped dead in her tracks, looking at Mallory with consternation.

"He's just not here," Mallory said, helplessly searching her pockets again. "Where can he be?"

"Do you suppose he tumbled out when that joker told you you had a spot on your skirt?" Mrs. Peebles asked.

Mallory looked stricken. "Oh gosh, maybe that's what happened. Oh, I don't believe it."

"We'll go back and search around by the shooting gallery," Mrs. Peebles said sensibly. "Now don't panic."

Slowly Mallory and Mrs. Peebles retraced their steps, their eyes glued to the ground. All these people, Mallory thought in despair, looking at the sneakered and sandaled feet of the carnival goers. Any of them could have stepped on Woody, crushing him flat.

"I think what we should do is go find Rudy," Mrs. Peebles said after ten minutes of fruitless hunting. "He knows the management here.

Maybe a search party could be organized or something."

Even more worried than she had been this afternoon when Woody had disappeared, Mallory followed along behind Mrs. Peebles, her eyes still searching the dusty, hard-packed ground.

"Wouldn't you think I could hold on to him?" she fretted. And then, unreasonably, she felt angry at Woody for being so easily lost. He was harder to keep track of than a ponytail holder or a pair of mittens in winter or the little stud earrings she wore in her newly pierced ears. Honestly, he was such an awful responsibility!

Halfway to the fortune-teller's tent they encountered a friend of Mrs. Peebles', a grey-haired man who was holding the hand of a little boy with a mop of curly blond hair.

"This is my grandson, Frankie," the friend said, looking down with a proud smile at the two-and-a-half-year-old standing beside him. Frankie was wearing bright-red shorts and had a pacifier in his mouth.

"Can you say hello to Mrs. Peebles and her little friend?" the grandfather asked, firmly removing the pacifier.

"Gimme!" Frankie protested, trying to grab it back.

"Big boys don't use pacifiers," the grandfather said. "Say hello to these folks."

Frankie looked sullen and remained silent. Mallory shifted her weight from one foot to the other and tried to catch Mrs. Peebles' eye to convey to her that this was no time to be standing around talking to babies.

"I think Frankie is a bit upset because he found this cute little doll a few minutes ago and then lost it," the grandfather explained. "Little guy in a business suit, even had a necktie. He was made out of some kind of material, vinyl maybe, that you'd swear was real skin. I should have stuck him in my pocket, but Frankie wanted to hold him."

Mallory and Mrs. Peebles exchanged a quick look of dismay.

"Where did you lose your dolly, honey, do you remember?" Mrs. Peebles asked, bending stiffly toward Frankie.

"He bited me, that dolly," Frankie said in an aggrieved voice.

"I don't think dollies bite," Mallory said, not at all sure that this particular dolly, trying to defend himself, had not sunk his teeth into his captor. She squatted down next to Frankie. "Could you show us where you lost the little man?" she asked.

"I didn't lose him," Frankie said, shaking his head slowly from side to side.

"Well then, where is he?" Mallory asked, staring earnestly into Frankie's eyes.

"I throwed him away," Frankie replied, turning to his grandfather. "I want my pac'fier," he said.

"Where did you throw him, dear?" Mrs. Peebles asked. She looked at the grandfather. "We think the little man might have been Mallory's here," she explained. "As a matter of fact we were looking for him when you came along."

"I knew I should have put him in my pocket," the grandfather said again. "Frankie, can you tell Grandpa where you dropped the dolly, sweetheart? He belongs to this little girl."

"I threwed him away, I told you," Frankie repeated, beginning to sound exasperated, "in a barrel."

"Where? What barrel?" Mallory glanced around wildly.

Frankie shrugged and looked down at his hand. "The dolly nipped me," he repeated, examining one of his fingers.

"I wonder if he means one of those trash barrels," the grandfather said, nodding at a large plastic container a few feet away. "There're a couple of them around here. Is that the one over there, Frankie, where you threw the doll?"

Frankie glowered at his grandfather. "I want my pac'fier."

The grandfather shook his head and looked apologetically at Mrs. Peebles and Mallory. "Sorry, folks," he said. "I'd try the trash barrels if I were you. Hope you find the doll." And he and Frankie moved off across the midway, arguing.

"The trouble is those trash cans are so large,"

Mrs. Peebles said, "and Mr. Sherman is so tiny, we might easily—"

"I'll start with the one over there," Mallory interrupted, already moving determinedly to the nearest barrel. "You can check out the one by the Tilt-A-Whirl."

"Righto," Mrs. Peebles said cooperatively, positioning her eyeglasses on her nose.

Mallory began sifting through the contents of her barrel. There were sticky paper cones on which cotton candy had been wrapped, bits of hot dog roll sodden with ketchup, Popsicle sticks, empty soda cans, Styrofoam cups, Styrofoam dishes with a few greasy French fries resting in them.

"Woody, are you in here?" she called every few seconds, willing him to answer. All at once she became aware of someone standing at her elbow. A boy was looking into the barrel with interest. "Who's Woody?" he asked curiously.

"Er, no one," Mallory said, peeking under a crushed paper napkin. "I was just thinking out loud."

The boy seemed unconvinced. "Can I look for him too?" he asked.

"No," Mallory told him impatiently. She was now at the bottom of the barrel and there was no Woody. Not really surprised that she had been unable to find him, she moved on to join Mrs. Peebles, who was still lifting bits of refuse from her barrel. She shook her head as Mallory approached to indicate she'd had no luck either.

"There's still that one down there by the entrance," she said, wiping away beads of sweat from her upper lip. "We might as well have a look."

"We're not going to find him, I know we're not," Mallory said. "And when Mom comes home tomorrow, I'll have to tell her I lost her husband."

"We haven't finished looking yet," Mrs. Peebles said. She was trying to sound briskly confident, but she looked pretty worried, Mallory thought, as they hurried toward the carnival entrance.

The barrel there had less refuse in it than

the other two, though someone had crammed wads of newspaper in it. She and Mrs. Peebles set to work together. Mallory's mind worked as feverishly as her fingers. As she sorted through newspaper, she imagined her mother, hysterical, shrieking and wringing her hands when told the news about Woody. Maybe she would no longer be able to bear the sight of her own daughter; maybe she would send Mallory off to boarding school in the fall. Pushing aside half a hamburger, still in its bun, Mallory quickly conjured up a picture of herself in an uninviting dormitory, sharing a cramped bedroom with some lively, self-confident girl who was not the least little bit homesick while she, Mallory, pined away for Jefferson Village.

But worse than that dreary picture was the thought of Woody, scared and lost, maybe even injured, struggling to get back to her from wherever he had fallen. And then a scrap of paper fluttered near her right hand and Woody's head appeared. On top of his head, like some kind of exotic turban, was a wad of pink bubblegum.

"Woody!" Mallory cried.

"Oh, thank heaven!" Mrs. Peebles said. "We thought you were a goner, Mr. Sherman, we really did."

"Woody, are you okay?" Mallory asked, weak with relief as she picked him from the garbage. "We were so worried!"

"*You* were worried," Woody said, slumping into the cradle of her hand. "You don't even know the meaning of the word. This giant child found me on the ground and began squeezing me. I had to bite his finger to make him let go.

"Ouch!" he said as Mallory pulled the gum from his hair. He looked up at her sternly. "No more sudden turns Mal, got it?" he said.

"Oh, then you did fall when I spun around before," Mallory said with chagrin. "I am such a jerk!"

"You just weren't thinking," Mrs. Peebles said forgivingly. "Now let's go find Rudy before disaster has a chance to strike again."

7

Rudy

THE FORTUNE-TELLER'S tent stood at the end of
the midway, beyond the food concession. On
a wooden easel in front of it was a poster that
showed a drawing of a woman with a bandanna around her head and big golden loops
in her ears. Her name, Madame Zorena, appeared above it, and the message "Unravel
the Secrets of the Future!" was printed below.

There was no sign, however, of the booth George Tucci had told Mrs. Peebles her husband would be occupying.

"I didn't think Rudy'd let himself be put way up here," she said. "He likes to be in the thick of things."

"Mrs. Peebles, this is not a hoax on your part, is it?" Woody asked accusingly, his head and shoulders visible above the gently curled fingers of Mallory's right hand. Darkness was falling, and it was beginning to be difficult to see him.

"Hoax?" Mrs. Peebles peered at him through her glasses.

"I mean is Rudy Peebles really at this carnival or not?"

Mrs. Peebles, without answering, cast a contemptuous look at Madame Zorena's poster. "If anyone knows where Rudy is, it'll be her," she said with a sniff. "Zorena's had her eye on that man for years, the hussy." She stepped to the entrance of the tent and pulled back the flap. The space beyond was dark, lit only by three flickering candles set in bottles on a table covered with a red cloth. In the center of the table was a crystal ball glittering with reflected candlelight. Behind it sat Madame Zorena in a bandanna and earrings. Mallory could see a long flowered skirt beneath the table.

"Please, I do not do zee group readings," Madame said in a throaty voice, shaking her head so that the loops in her ears glinted in the candle glow. "One of you must step outside."

Mrs. Peebles peered at the seated figure more closely. Madame Zorena looked uneasy and raised one large hand to her face, as though trying to hide it from such intense scrutiny.

"Rudy, is that you?" Mrs. Peebles demanded.

There was a moment of silence, then "Ssh!" The figure behind the table raised a cautionary finger. "The whole carnival will hear you, Loretta."

"Would you mind telling me what you are doing dressed up in Zorena's outfit?" Mrs. Peebles demanded.

Mr. Peebles scowled. "Zorena came down

with a virus yesterday, and the carnival manager asked me to fill in for her because he feels
she's such a drawing card. Never mind about
my show," he said, sounding highly offended,
"but I'll tell you, a magician draws a bigger
audience any day of the week. Honestly, I'm
treated like a second-class citizen around
here." He turned his attention to Mallory.
"And who might you be, my dear?" he asked.

"I'm Mallory Watson, and my step—" Mallory began.

"Actually I'm not bad with a crystal ball,"
Mr. Peebles said. "If you'd care to have your
fortune told, I'll give you a full reading for ten
percent off."

"We're here on business," said Woody in a
small but clear voice. He signaled to Mallory
to place him on the table.

Mr. Peebles' eyes nearly popped out of his
head. "What in the world, or should I say who
in the world—is that?" he gasped, pulling off
his bandanna as he leaned across the table for
a closer look.

"Rudy, we think it was that compound of

yours, you know, your Lose It Now, that has done a job on Woody Sherman here," Mrs. Peebles told her husband. "Naturally the poor man's very upset."

Mr. Peebles had eyes only for Woody. "This is absolutely incredible," he said. "I never imagined my little powder could be so potent." He glanced briefly at Mrs. Peebles. "I assume he ate one of your candies."

"That's right." Mrs. Peebles nodded.

"And you used only a pinch of Lose It Now in the candy?"

"Well, I might have put in just the tiniest bit more," Mrs. Peebles conceded.

"Well, there you go," Mr. Peebles said, getting up from his chair. "The woman obviously used the wrong proportion in her recipe. Really, Loretta," he said, giving her a reproachful look. "How very irresponsible of you." He moved around to the other side of the table. "May I hold you, sir?" he asked respectfully. But Woody gave him such a fierce look Mr. Peebles quickly withdrew his outstretched hand.

"The point here is not how much of this wacky powder Mrs. Peebles used in her candy but what you can now do to help me," Woody said, trying, Mallory could tell, to take charge of the situation.

"Hmm, you're thinking of my Add 'n Inch, I suppose?" Mr. Peebles said, scratching his chin thoughtfully.

"Add 'n Inch?" Woody repeated. "I have no idea—"

"It's something I came up with several months ago," Mr. Peebles said modestly, "designed for folks who wish, for whatever reason, to add a few inches to their height."

"Oh, do you think it could help my stepfather?" Mallory asked eagerly.

Mr. Peebles studied her for a moment. "It certainly wouldn't hurt to give it a try," he said. "I haven't done extensive testing on Add 'n Inch, I'll admit, but it worked wonders on my ficus plant."

"Would you believe that crazy thing grew three feet almost overnight!" Mrs. Peebles informed Mallory and Woody.

"It was odd," Mr. Peebles said. "Nothing happened at all when I watered around the roots, but when I sprinkled a bit of the compound over the leaves, that's when we got results."

"It was a shame about those leaves though," Mrs. Peebles said.

"What about them?" Woody asked grimly.

"Well, some shriveled," Mr. Peebles admitted. "I'm still working on the problem of leaf retention, but as you're not a plant, Mr. Sherman, that part shouldn't worry you too much. Quite frankly, I think Add 'n Inch is our only option."

"Do you have some here with you?" Mallory asked.

"Of course not." Mr. Peebles gave her an amused look. "It's at home in my laboratory," he said grandly, pronouncing the word in the English way, with the accent on the second syllable. He unknotted the shawl wrapped about his shoulders and stepped out of his long skirt, revealing grubby-looking jeans beneath it.

"I may be fired for leaving my post like this," he said, "but as a man of science, I know where my duty lies."

"May I assist you from the table, sir?" he asked Woody.

"No," Woody said. "Only Mallory may touch me."

Feeling flattered, Mallory lifted him from the table.

"Follow me," Mr. Peebles instructed, leading the way from the tent. "With any luck at all, Mr. Sherman, we'll soon have your little problem solved. No pun intended, sir."

Woody looked at Mallory. "What do you think?" he asked.

"I think we've got to go for it," she said. She crossed the fingers of her left hand for luck and said a silent prayer as she put him back into her pocket.

8

Add 'n Inch

MRS. PEEBLES DROVE somewhat more compe-
tently with Mr. Peebles up ahead of her as
a guide in his yellow car. Mallory kept her
fingers crossed all the way to his house; when
they pulled up in front of it, she climbed
from the car and immediately cast her eyes
skyward, looking for a shooting star on which
to make a quick wish for Woody's recovery.

But all the stars overhead, glowing like so many little lanterns, remained steadfastly in place.

On the dark lawn a small ruby light blinked sleepily on and off. Mallory was about to ask what it was and then realized it was the left eye of the gnome winking at them. Mr. Peebles, taking no notice, drew a key from his pocket and opened the front door. He snapped on an overhead light, and Mallory found herself in a narrow hall, empty except for a grandfather clock with a smiling moon painted on its face. The moon had eyes and lips that began to move as she looked at it. A voice that sounded like a scratchy recording from within the clock case spoke. "Seven o'clock and all's well," it chanted. "The wind's in the west and blowing like—"

"Rudy!" Mrs. Peebles said sharply. "You've got to do something about that clock."

"Tsk, tsk," Mr. Peebles muttered, giving the moon face a disapproving glance. "Watch your language, please." He peered down at his wristwatch. "And I have nine twenty-five."

"Also the wind doesn't seem to be blowing from any direction at all," Mallory pointed out, studying the cheerful moon face. "It's perfectly calm outside."

On a hunch she asked, "Is the clock another of your brother Randall's inventions?"

"Why yes," Mr. Peebles said, looking at her in surprise. "Do you know Randall?"

Mallory shook her head.

"He runs The Clockery over in Springdale. If you ever have a clock that needs repairing, he's the fellow to take it to."

Mallory felt Woody stir in her pocket. "Don't you dare ever go near that place, Mallory," he said sternly.

Mr. Peebles, after opening a door at the end of the hall, flicked on a wall switch and led the way down a flight of steps to the basement. Beneath a naked bulb hanging from the ceiling was a long laboratory table. Mallory could see all sorts of equipment arranged on top—a test-tube stand filled with test tubes, a Bunsen burner, tongs, a small scale, a mortar and pestle, cylinders, and on a metal tripod a flask of bright-purple liquid. From one of the cylinders a silver bubble suddenly rose and burst loudly.

"What's that?" Woody asked suspiciously, working his way to the top of Mallory's pocket.

"Moonseed," Mr. Peebles said briefly, "mashed together with certain other substances."

"Does it have something to do with Add 'n Inch?" Mallory asked.

"Oh dear, no," Mr. Peebles chuckled, but made no attempt to explain the moonseed's use. He stepped up to the table, rubbing his hands together. "Now then," he said, "we'll just mix up a little something for you, Mr. Sherman, and see what happens."

This is it, Mallory thought, drawing in a long breath. She and Woody and Mrs. Peebles watched, transfixed, as Mr. Peebles lifted from its holder a test tube containing a small amount of clear liquid. He inserted the tube into a metal clamp, lit his Bunsen burner, and then held the tube over it to heat.

"How long—" Mrs. Peebles began, but Mr. Peebles put up a hand to quiet her.

"I'm counting," he said tensely.

After several moments of silence, Mr. Peebles poured the contents of the test tube into the flask of purple liquid. From a drawer in the table he extracted a plastic bag filled with red powder. He sprinkled a little of this in the flask and immediately there were a series of mini explosions that sounded like someone snapping bubble-gum bubbles. The liquid changed in color to green, then to yellow and back to purple.

"May I ask you to put Mr. Sherman on the table here?" Mr. Peebles asked Mallory, indicating a spot next to the flask. "I must make certain vital computations. What is your normal height, sir?" he inquired, looking closely at Woody.

"Five eleven," Woody said with a nervous gulp.

"Former weight?" Mr. Peebles picked up a pad and pencil lying on the table.

"One sixty-five."

Mr. Peebles briskly uncoiled a tape measure lying behind a white ceramic dish.

"Three and one eighth inches," he murmured, holding it lightly against Woody. "And we need your present weight." All at once he swooped Woody up and put him in the pan of the scale.

"Hey, wait a minute," Woody protested.

"Four and one quarter ounces," Mr. Peebles announced, consulting the pointer beneath the pan.

He set Woody back on the table and began scribbling figures on his pad. "It is vital to administer just the proper dosage if Mr. Sherman is to regain his normal size," he explained when he had finished. "It would be awkward, would it not, if he were to shoot up to ten or eleven feet?"

"Very awkward," Woody muttered. "Peebles, do you think we have a pretty good chance of restoring me to my proper size? I'd like to know going into this whether—"

"I am reasonably confident that we can," Mr. Peebles said, "though of course we are engaged in a bit of pioneering here. Add 'n Inch is a new product. There is always the possibility that—" Seeing the look on Woody's face, he broke off his sentence and began rummaging in the table drawer again. Mallory stepped closer to see what he kept in there besides the mysterious red powder. She saw a jumble of paper clips, rubber bands, discount grocery coupons, several sticks of chewing gum, pencils, and an address book.

"Ah, here it is," Mr. Peebles said, drawing out a Coca-Cola bottle cap. "I think Mr. Sherman will be able to sip quite well from this." With care, he poured a few drops of the purple liquid from the flask into the bottle cap and held it out to Woody.

"Okay, my friend, chugalug," he said.

Mallory and Mr. and Mrs. Peebles stared at Woody as he slowly raised the bottle cap to his lips.

"Here goes," he said, closing his eyes and taking a long swig. He opened them and looked thoughtfully at the ceiling. "Tastes like grape," he said. He finished off the drink and laid the bottle cap on the table. He looked expectantly at Mr. Peebles, who continued to stare at him. Everybody waited in anxious silence. Nothing happened.

"We must give it a chance," Mr. Peebles said at length.

"Well, but how long will that be?" Woody demanded. "I shrank in a matter of minutes—there was no waiting around for that to happen, I can tell you." He looked to Mallory for confirmation.

"Oh by the way, if Add 'n Inch works for Mr. Sherman, can I have some for Alice?" Mrs. Peebles asked. "Poor little thing, she's the laughingstock of the neighborhood, at least among the other cats."

"How can you tell?" Mallory asked curiously.

"I've seen the smirks on their faces, the amusement in their eyes," Mrs. Peebles said, nodding wisely. "Of course you have to be really into cats to notice."

"Nothing's happening," Woody reminded them in a bleak voice. He looked down at his legs, then stretched out his arms. "Do you think my fingers are maybe looking a little longer, Mallory?" he asked.

"Not really," she told him, trying not to sound as disappointed as she felt.

Mr. Peebles reached for an empty test tube and poured some Add 'n Inch into it. From the table drawer he withdrew a cork, which he placed in the neck of the test tube.

"If there is no improvement by the time you get home," he said, handing the container to Mallory, "give him half of this dose. If there is still no improvement, call me in the morning."

"I can't see what good all your measuring and figuring did," Woody said testily. "If you want my opinion, Mr. Peebles, I don't think you have a clue as to how your crazy concoctions work."

"Trust me, dear boy," Mr. Peebles said. "Rudy Peebles is a lot smarter than he may look."

"I'm doomed," Woody said, and when Mallory tucked him into her pocket, he sank limply to the bottom.

9

Mallory's Triumph

"NOW REMEMBER, I want to be told what happens with Mr. Sherman too," Mrs. Peebles said when, fifteen minutes later, she let Mallory off in her driveway.

"Don't worry," she added, looking at Mallory's gloomy face. "Mr. Peebles is a very able scientist no matter what anyone says."

"You believe that, you believe anything,"

Woody mumbled disconsolately.

As soon as they got into the house, Mallory sat Woody on the kitchen counter and ran upstairs for another teacup from the cupboard in the dollhouse.

"You know what I'm thinking, Mallory?" Woody said, watching her fill it over the kitchen sink with Add 'n Inch.

"What?" she asked.

"That if I'm to go through life as a three-inch freak, maybe I'd better get into show business like Mrs. Peebles suggested."

"No!" Mallory said in horror.

"But how else can I earn the money to take care of you and your mom?" He glared at her fiercely. "I can hardly argue a case in court the way I am now."

"Drink," Mallory ordered, not knowing what else to say to him. He tilted his head back and drained the cup. She saw him steal a glance at himself, checking for growth.

"Please take me up to bed," he said after five minutes produced no visible change. "I'm exhausted."

Sorrowfully Mallory carried him to the doll-house.

"You call me in the night if you feel yourself growing even a tiny bit, okay?" she urged.

"I think we'd better forget about any change in my condition," Woody said gruffly. In the guest room he climbed into his dollhouse bed and pulled the quilt up over his head. Mallory sat down on the floor and gazed into the dollhouse, willing Woody to grow. After a few minutes she became uneasy because he was lying so still. She got up and peered into his bed. Was he even breathing beneath the quilt? It was hard to tell. She reached in and pulled the cover back. Thank goodness, his left shoulder beneath Mr. Hemingway's rumpled suit was rising and falling gently. He was sound asleep. Mallory went to her own room and wandered to the mirror over the bureau.

"This is going to be some awful night," she said to her reflection, and decided then and there that she wouldn't even try to sleep, at least not yet. She got into her pajamas and carried her pillow and the blanket at the foot of the bed downstairs to the den. She turned on the TV and lay down on the couch. Several cowboys rode toward her across a bleak-looking plain. Mallory was not much into westerns, but she needed company and the cowboys were probably about as good as she was going to find.

She drifted in and out of sleep. The cowboys rode away and were replaced by a broadly smiling talk-show host. Mallory dozed on, awakening sometime in the night to a black-and-white movie in which the heroine was dressed in a hoopskirt. She slept some more, and the next time she awoke it was light out. On the TV a church choir in red robes was singing an unfamiliar hymn. She sat up groggily and turned off the TV.

Out of habit, certainly not because she was hungry, she padded down the hall to the kitchen. The first thing she saw was the test tube lying on the counter It still contained a few drops of Add 'n Inch. And as she stared at it, Mr. Peebles' words of last night went through her head: "Nothing happened when I watered around the roots of my ficus," he had said, "but when I sprinkled a bit over the leaves, that's when we got results."

Mallory hesitated for a moment, then picked up the test tube in her hand and carried it to the guest room. Woody was still in bed. He had kicked off his covers during the night and was lying with his knees drawn up and his face turned toward the wall. Even in sleep he looked like someone who had given up. Mallory leaned into the dollhouse and dumped the Add 'n Inch from the test tube onto his head. He awoke with a gasp and struggled into a sitting position. "What the heck's going on?" he spluttered as purple drops ran down into his eyes.

"Did you just pour water on me, Mallory?" he asked reproachfully, wiping at his face with both hands.

"I'm sorry, Woody," she apologized. "I thought maybe if I poured the Add 'n Inch over you, like you were a plant, it might work better than if you drank it."

"Well, now I'm completely soaked," he said

angrily, "and I certainly don't have anything else I can put on."

"I'll get you a towel," Mallory said, and hurried to the bathroom. The bath sheet on the towel rack was definitely too big for him, and even the hand towel next to it seemed too large. A washcloth would be better, she thought, reaching into the cupboard below the sink.

At that moment, a sound like wood splintering, followed by a wild whoop, issued from the guest room. Startled, Mallory rushed back down the hall. Standing in the center of the guest room, the pink quilted bedspread clutched to him, was Woody. He was no longer a tiny dollhouse figure but a full-grown, triumphant Woody, looking even taller in fact than she remembered him.

Now it was Mallory's turn to let out a whoop. She ran across the room, relief and joy flooding over her. Woody caught her in the arm he had untangled from the bedspread and gave her a great big hug, the first he had ever really given her.

"Mal, you are a genius," he told her. "I do think it was your pouring that crazy stuff of Peebles' over my head that did the trick." He hugged her again and stepped over to the mirror.

"It's a miracle," he marveled, turning this way and that, flexing a wrist, staring at his bare feet with a rapt expression.

"You look just great," Mallory told him. "Better than I even remember you."

Woody glanced back at the dollhouse. "I'm sorry about that, Mal." He motioned with his chin at the red roof, which, she noticed for the first time, was hanging lopsidedly over the second floor as though it had just been through a cyclone.

"It was my head that did the damage when I started to grow. A couple of nails and the roof will be as good as new. I'll fix it for you later, when I've calmed down a little," he promised. Mal smiled tolerantly as he turned back to the mirror for another look at himself. He'd have trouble with the job, you could bet on it, but that was okay. Not everyone was a whiz with a hammer and nails.

Downstairs the doorbell rang.

"Who can that be?" Woody turned from the mirror with a worried frown and then relaxed. "I forgot," he said with a grin. "I don't have to hide anymore. Whoever's down there, I'm ready for them."

"Not wrapped up in a bedspread you're not," Mallory told him, and ran to answer the door.

On the front steps stood Mr. and Mrs. Peebles.

"How's the patient?" Mr. Peebles asked in a sickroom half whisper.

"He's himself again," Mallory announced breathlessly.

"No!" Mrs. Peebles looked at her husband, her face wreathed in smiles.

"Well, can you beat that!" Mr. Peebles exclaimed, and then added hastily, "Not that I had any serious doubts about Add 'n Inch, of course."

"Come in and see him for yourself," Mallory invited, holding the screen door open.

As the Peebleses stepped into the hall,

Woody came down the stairs in the khaki trousers and striped shirt he had been wearing on Friday night.

"Is it the same fellow?" Mrs. Peebles asked, staring at him. "Why yes, I believe it is," she said, answering her own question. "I recognize the hair."

"Congratulations, sir," Mr. Peebles said, walking toward Woody with his hand extended.

But Woody kept both his own resolutely thrust in his pants pocket. "Mr. and Mrs. Peebles," he said in a very serious voice, "I need hardly say how overjoyed I am to be myself again. And I know if it were not for your help, Rudy, I'd still be mouse size. But those two products of yours, Lose It Now and Add 'n Inch, they've got to go. I must have your assurance that they will both be disposed of, and I mean right away."

"Oh, you have my word on that, Mr. Sherman," Mr. Peebles assured him without hesitation. "I'm putting inventions behind me and, as a matter-of-fact, show business as well."

Woody gave him a skeptical look. "What

will you do, then?" he asked.

"Last night Loretta and I decided to reunite and move to Florida," Mr. Peebles announced. "I've often toyed with the idea of opening a bait shop. I'm pretty good with my hands, and I think I'll make lures on the side—you know, those things with bright feathers and eyes to attract the fish."

"And I'll go into candy making full-time," Mrs. Peebles said happily. "I'll sell my goods in Rudy's shop."

"Well, it sounds like an ideal arrangement," Woody said, "if you're sure you can put anything remotely having to do with growth and weight control right out of the picture."

"No problem," Mr. Peebles told him. "Although," he said, "I have been working on a product I call Add a Pound. It might have some potential for the fishing industry. I mean, if a thirty-pound trout were to be developed for example—"

"No!" Woody and Mallory said in one voice.

"You're right, you're right," Mr. Peebles

agreed. "Much better plan just to stick to the bait shop." He glanced at his watch. "I think Loretta and I have taken up enough of your time. We must be on our way."

Everybody shook hands all around, and as Mallory opened the front door, she saw, much to her joy, her mother's car pulling into the driveway.

"Mom's early!" she exclaimed. "She wasn't supposed to be home till noon."

"I was anxious to get back to you guys," Mrs. Sherman explained when, after greeting the Peebleses on the front walk with a puzzled smile, she hugged Mallory and Woody and set her suitcase down in the hall. "Why was Mrs. Peebles here with her husband?" she asked Mallory.

"She came to say good-bye," Mallory said quickly. "She's going to Florida with Mr. Peebles."

"Oh well, that's nice that those two have gotten back together," her mother said. "We'll miss her."

She turned to Woody. "How did everything

go?" she inquired lightly. "No major problems?"

Woody and Mallory exchanged a glance.

"A few," Woody said, "but nothing this smart daughter of yours couldn't solve." He gave Mallory's ponytail a gentle tug.

"I tried to do my best," Mallory said modestly.

Mrs. Sherman gave her a grateful but baffled look. "Why do I get the feeling you and Woody know something I don't?" she asked.

"A mom's intuition, I guess," Woody said with a shrug. "I'm starving. Who will join me at Patsy's Pantry for breakfast?"

"Me! That's my favorite place," Mallory said enthusiastically.

"I would still like to know what's going on here," Mrs. Sherman said. "Something, I can feel it in my bones."

Woody put one arm around her, the other around Mallory. "Mal and I will clue you in over French toast," he promised.